Dear Parents:

Congratulations! Your child is taking the first steps on an exciting journey. The destination? Independent reading!

STEP INTO READING® will help your child get there. The program offers five steps to reading success. Each step includes fun stories and colorful art or photographs. In addition to original fiction and books with favorite characters, there are Step into Reading Non-Fiction Readers, Phonics Readers and Boxed Sets, Sticker Readers, and Comic Readers—a complete literacy program with something to interest every child.

Learning to Read, Step by Step!

Ready to Read   Preschool–Kindergarten
• big type and easy words • rhyme and rhythm • picture clues
For children who know the alphabet and are eager to begin reading.

Reading with Help   Preschool–Grade 1
• basic vocabulary • short sentences • simple stories
For children who recognize familiar words and sound out new words with help.

Reading on Your Own   Grades 1–3
• engaging characters • easy-to-follow plots • popular topics
For children who are ready to read on their own.

Reading Paragraphs   Grades 2–3
• challenging vocabulary • short paragraphs • exciting stories
For newly independent readers who read simple sentences with confidence.

Ready for Chapters   Grades 2–4
• chapters • longer paragraphs • full-color art
For children who want to take the plunge into chapter books but still like colorful pictures.

STEP INTO READING® is designed to give every child a successful reading experience. The grade levels are only guides; children will progress through the steps at their own speed, developing confidence in their reading.

Remember, a lifetime love of reading starts with a single step!

Step into Reading, Random House, and the Random House colophon are registered trademarks of
Random House LLC.

Visit us on the Web!
StepIntoReading.com
randomhousekids.com

Educators and librarians, for a variety of teaching tools, visit us at RHTeachersLibrarians.com

ISBN 978-0-7364-3318-1 (trade) — ISBN 978-0-7364-8170-0 (lib. bdg.) — ISBN 978-0-7364-3319-8 (ebook)

Printed in the United States of America   10 9 8 7 6 5 4 3 2 1

DISNEY · PIXAR
INSIDE OUT

Welcome to Headquarters

By Apple Jordan

Illustrated by the Disney Storybook Art Team

Random House 🏠 New York

Meet Riley!

She is eleven years old.

I'm Joy,
one of Riley's Emotions.
I live in Headquarters
inside Riley's mind.
My job is to make sure
Riley is happy.
Let me show you around.

Riley is a very happy girl.
She has great friends
and a loving family.

Riley's memories are stored
in spheres.
Happy memories are yellow!

Riley has other Emotions, too.
Anger makes sure everything
in Riley's life is fair.
Fear's job is
to keep Riley safe.
Disgust keeps Riley
away from gross things.

This is Sadness.

I am not sure what she does.

Riley has a great life!

And when Riley is happy,
we are happy.

Riley has five
Islands of Personality.
They make her
who she is.

There is Family Island,
Honesty Island, Hockey Island,
Friendship Island,
and Goofball Island.

Here comes the Train of Thought!
It drops off Riley's daydreams
every morning.

Let's climb aboard
to see the rest of Riley's mind.

These are the Forgetters.
They work in Long Term Memory.
They decide which memories
Riley does not need anymore.

The Forgetters vacuum up the old memories and send them to the Memory Dump.

The Memory Dump
is where old memories go.
Nothing comes back
from the Memory Dump.

This is how we make room
for Riley's new memories.

Meet Bing Bong.

He was Riley's imaginary
friend when she was little.
They used to go on
adventures together.

Riley has forgotten
about Bing Bong.
Sometimes he gets sad
and cries candy.
But he still loves Riley.

Bing Bong's favorite place
in Riley's mind
is Imagination Land.

Trophy Town, French Fry Forest, and Cloud Town are all parts of Imagination Land.

Riley's dreams are made
at Dream Productions.

Look!

It's Rainbow Unicorn.

She is the star

of Riley's best dreams.

I am her biggest fan!

Should I go say hi?

The cast and crew prepare
for Riley's next dream.
The writers write the scripts.
The actors put on costumes.
"Action!" yells the dream director.

Everyone works hard
to make sure Riley
has happy dreams.
Happy dreams help Riley sleep.
But sometimes a nightmare
wakes her up.

Riley's biggest fears are kept
in her Subconscious.
Two guards keep watch
in front of the gate.

The basement stairs,
Grandma's vacuum cleaner,
and Jangles the birthday clown
are all locked up here.

As you can see,
Riley's mind is a busy place.

As Emotions, it's our job
to take care of her.

After all, a good day turns
into a good week,
which turns into a good year,
which turns into a good life!
That is what we all want
for Riley!